A Day at the Trout Farm

Heather Hammonds

Contents

Chapter 1	**Fish for Dinner**	2
Chapter 2	**A Farm for Fish**	4
Chapter 3	**About Trout**	6
Chapter 4	**In the Hatchery**	8
Chapter 5	**Small Fry**	10
Chapter 6	**Growing Bigger**	12
Chapter 7	**Ready to Eat**	16
Chapter 8	**Fishing for Trout**	18
Chapter 9	**Our Trout Chart**	22
Glossary and Index		24

Chapter 1

Fish for Dinner

I like to eat fish.
Dad likes to eat fish too.

We have fish for dinner every week.

Trout is our favourite fish.
We went fishing at a trout farm.
Dad helped me catch some trout!

I learned a lot about trout farming at the trout farm.

Fishy Fact

There are different kinds of trout. This trout is called a **rainbow trout**.

Chapter 2

A Farm for Fish

Dad took me to a big trout farm.
The farm was in the mountains.

There were lots of ponds at the farm.
The ponds were full of rainbow trout.

trout pond

The trout farm was near a river.
The cold, clean water in the trout ponds came from the river.

Fishy Fact

Trout need very clean water to live and grow.

Chapter 3

About Trout

At the trout farm I learned:

- Trout live on trout farms and in lakes and rivers.

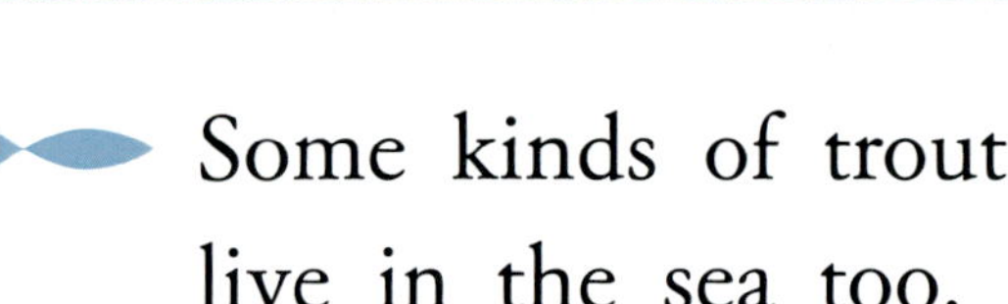

- Some kinds of trout live in the sea too.

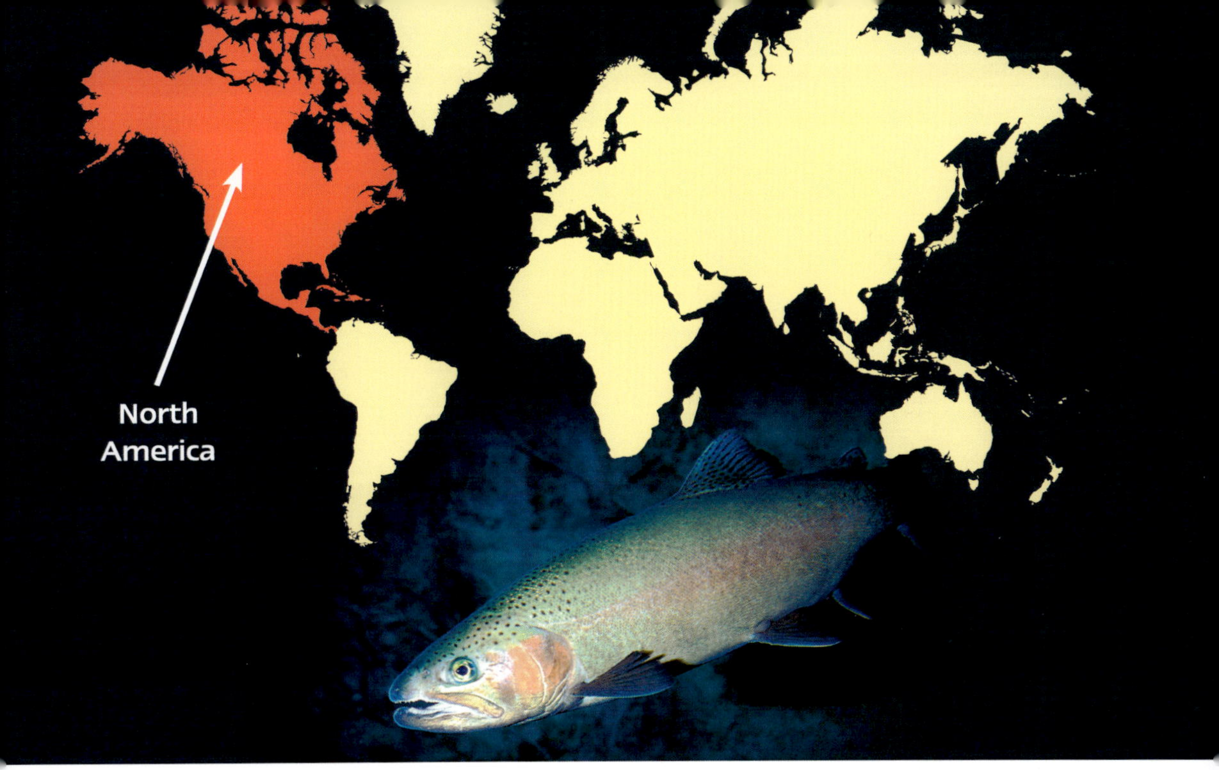

North
America

Rainbow trout first lived in parts of **North America**. Then people took their eggs to other countries.

Now rainbow trout are found all around the world.

Fishy Fact

Trout like to eat small insects and other fish or water animals.

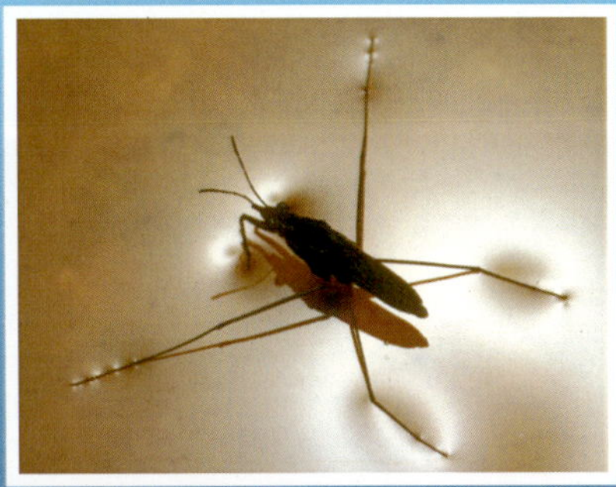

Chapter 4

In the Hatchery

Dad and I saw the **hatchery** at the trout farm.

We saw lots of tiny trout eggs in special **incubators.** We could see the eyes of the baby trout inside some of the eggs!

an alevin

When baby trout hatch out of their eggs, they are called **alevins**.
At first alevins do not need to eat.
They get all their food from their **yolk sacs**.

Fishy Fact

Trout eggs are called 'eyed eggs' when the eyes of baby trout can be seen inside them.

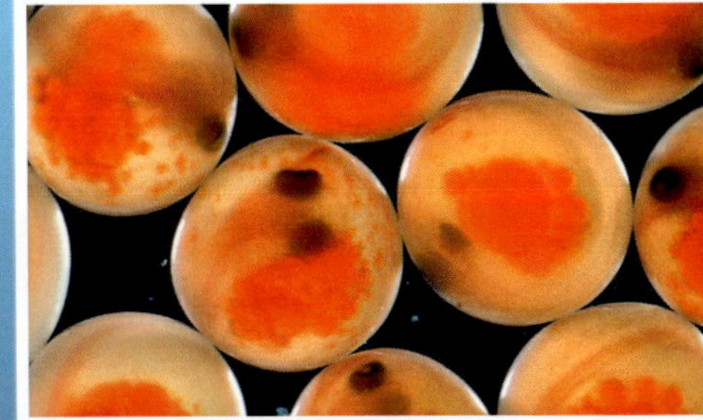

Chapter 5

Small Fry

Baby trout grow very quickly.
We saw some baby trout
that were bigger than alevins.
Their yolk sacs were gone.
They had become **fry**.

The fry were swimming around in long tanks. The fry are fed special trout food every day.

Fishy Fact

Trout at trout farms are given special food to help them grow well.

Chapter 6

Growing Bigger

Next we looked inside some different tanks.
We saw hundreds of little trout!

The trout were bigger than the fry.
They had become **fingerlings**.

We learned that most of the fingerlings would stay at the trout farm.

But some of the fingerlings would go to other trout farms, or to lakes, or dams.

Fishy Fact

Trout from some trout farms are let go into lakes and rivers.

Then we went to a pond full of trout.
We threw some trout food into the water.
Lots of trout jumped up to get the food.

The trout were one year old.
They were much bigger than the fingerlings.

We looked at some other ponds.
We saw bigger trout and smaller trout.

Fishy Fact

Bigger and smaller trout are kept in different ponds at trout farms.

Chapter 7

Ready to Eat

When the trout have grown big,
it is time to catch them.
We learned that most of the trout
are sold to markets and restaurants.

Some of the trout are kept at the trout farm. They are sold at the farm shop.

We went into the farm shop and looked around.

Fishy Fact

Trout must be kept very cold, to keep them fresh.

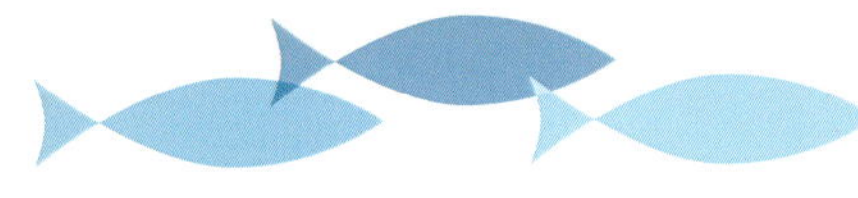

Chapter 8

Fishing for Trout

At the farm shop, we got some fishing rods and some **bait**.

We went fishing in a special pond at the trout farm.

Dad put some bait on my hook.
Then we put our fishing lines into the pond.

We waited to catch our trout.

Fishy Fact

Many trout farms have special ponds where visitors can go fishing.

While we were fishing
Dad told me about other trout farms.
At some trout farms trout are kept in:

- long raceways

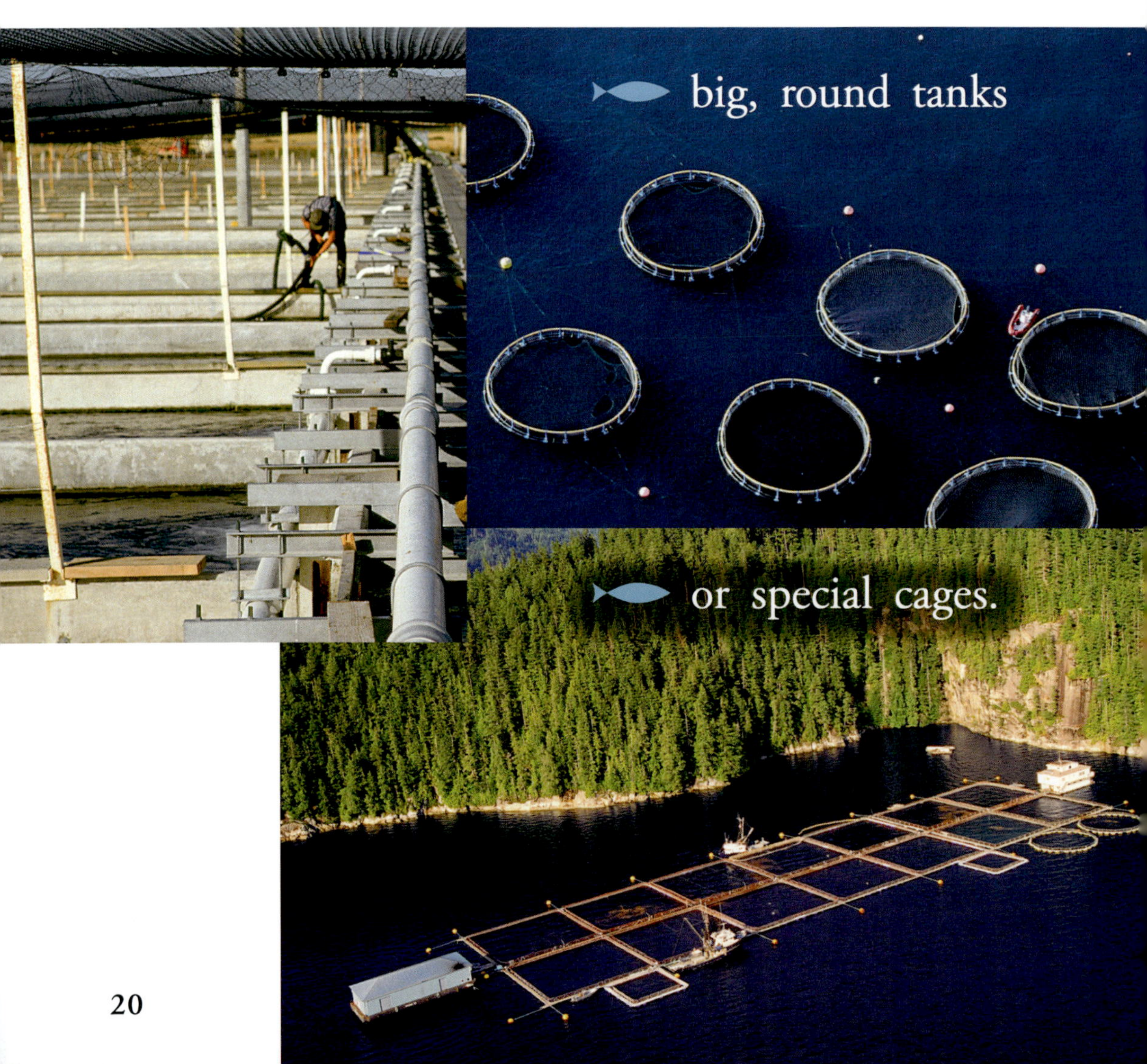

- big, round tanks
- or special cages.

At last I caught
some trout.

Dad did not catch
any trout.
I said he could have
some of mine!

Fishy Fact

The largest trout live in lakes and seas.
They grow much bigger than trout at trout farms.

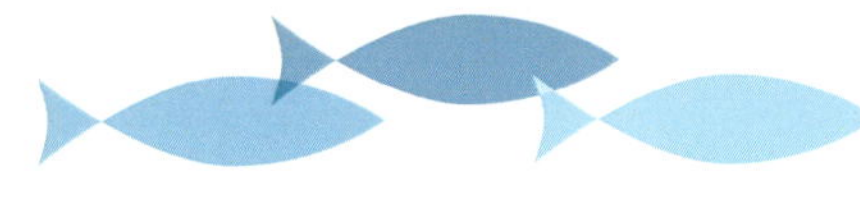

Chapter 9

Our Trout Chart

We had lots of fun at the trout farm. I made a chart, so I will remember what I saw there.

trout eggs

alevins

fry

Fishy Fact

Trout come from the same family of fish as salmon.

Glossary

alevins	baby trout that have just hatched
bait	fish food, used to catch fish
fingerlings	young trout that are older and bigger than alevins or fry
fry	baby trout that are older and bigger than alevins
hatchery	a place where baby trout are hatched from eggs
incubators	special tanks where trout eggs grow and hatch
North America	a place in the northern part of the world
raceways	long concrete ponds used at fish farms
rainbow trout	a kind of trout with a shiny pink strip on its sides
yolk sacs	small yellow lumps on new-born alevins that hold food for them

Index

alevins 9–10
eggs 7–9
fingerlings 12–13
fishing 3, 18–20
fry 10–12
hatchery 8
incubators 8
ponds 4–5, 14–15, 18–19
rainbow trout 3–4, 7
tanks 11, 20